This edition published by
W H Smith Publishers, Canada.

Produced by
Twin Books
15 Sherwood Place
Greenwich, CT 06830
USA

ISBN 0-88665-648-6

Printed in Hong Kong

ARMSTRONG THE ROBOT

Twin Books

B. Mitchell

The train was slowly making its way around the mountain when Scrooge McDuck and his nephews Huey, Dewey, and Louie heard a screeching sound. The train came to a sudden stop, and Scrooge and the boys found themselves thrown to the back of the car.

"What happened?" asked Huey.

"I'm goin' to find out," answered Scrooge.

They climbed out of the car and ran to the front of the train. It was a good thing the engineer had stopped the train, because they had almost crashed into a huge pile of rocks.

"Now how are we goin' to continue our journey?" wondered Scrooge aloud.

"Call Launchpad, Unca Scrooge," said Louie. "I'll bet he can get us out of this."

"Do you really think he can help?" asked Scrooge.

"Sure!" said Dewey.

The engineer let Scrooge use the train's radio to call Launchpad. "We're in trouble, Launchpad," said Scrooge. "Come to Mount Helena right away."

"Right, Mr. McD! I'm on my way!"

Before long, Launchpad's plane landed on the roof of the train. Then he jumped down, and started trying to move the rocks, but it was no use. They were just too heavy.

"It's impossible!" sighed Launchpad, after trying to move the rocks. "Twenty men couldn't move even one of these!"

Suddenly they heard a helicopter coming. It landed nearby.

"It's Gyro!" cried Huey. "Look what he's brought!"

"I heard your radio call for help and thought you might need us," said Gyro. Then he turned to his robot.

"Armstrong," said Gyro, "move those rocks."

The robot cleared away the rocks in no time, surprising everyone.

The next day Gyro and Launchpad went to Scrooge's house. While Launchpad and Scrooge's nephews played with a toy robot, Gyro explained what Armstrong could do for Scrooge.

"He does everything," said Gyro. "He washes dishes and clothes, dusts, keeps the house clean, cooks and sets the table. He can also do bookkeeping, drive a car—in short, he can do anything you ask without getting tired, or making a mistake."

"And he works for free!" added Scrooge.

Scrooge loved his new robot.

"I won't be needing you anymore, Launchpad," said Scrooge, walking him to the door.

"But, I've always been your pilot!" said Launchpad.

"I know, but times change," said Scrooge. "I'll probably be letting my butler go, too. I'll call if I need you." And with that, Launchpad found himself on the street.

Soon Armstrong was taking care of all the housework, and ran Scrooge's businesses besides. Scrooge fired thousands of office workers because he didn't need them anymore. In fact, when Scrooge went to work, there was nothing for him to do, either. The robot had done it all—and done it better than Scrooge could himself, without making any mistakes.

One day, Scrooge went to his money bin and found Armstrong emptying it out.

"What are you doin'? Where did you put me money? Thief!" cried Scrooge. "You're fired!"

The robot grabbed Scrooge by the neck and carried him, kicking and screaming, to Gyro's house.

Armstrong locked Gyro and Scrooge up in a small room with an electrified doorway, so they couldn't escape.

"What is it you want?" asked Scrooge, furiously.

"To rule the world," said Armstrong. "I'm smarter than you, and now I have your money to put my plan into action."

"You're crazy," said Gyro. "You'll never get away with it!"

When Scrooge's nephews returned from school, they were surprised to find Armstrong aiming a weapon at them.
"He's got a laser gun!" yelled Huey.
"What has he done with Unca Scrooge?" asked Dewey.
"I don't know, but we need help. Let's get Launchpad!"
The brothers raced to Launchpad's house.

They found Launchpad packing. "Hi, kids," he said sadly. "Did you come to say goodbye?"

"Goodbye? Are you going somewhere?"

"Sure. Mr. McD doesn't need me since he got Armstrong."

"That's why we've come," said Huey. "The robot went crazy and shot at us. We don't know what's happened to Unca Scrooge. What can we do?"

"Let's go find Gyro," said Launchpad, taking charge. "He's the one who made that monster."

"There's no time to lose," said Huey, running to the door.

"Wait," said Louie. "We'll never get there in time on our bikes."

"Dewey is right," agreed Launchpad. "We'll use my plane."

Soon they were flying to Gyro's, not knowing that it was the very place Armstrong had chosen for his base. In a few minutes, they landed loudly on the roof of Gyro's lab, unaware that the robot had seen them land.

"The plane is losing fuel!" cried Dewey.

"That's only water," said Launchpad. "I've been working as a firefighter lately, and there's still water in the tank. It probably spilled when we landed," he said, knocking at the lab door.

Armstrong came out, ready for a fight. Launchpad took one look and ran.

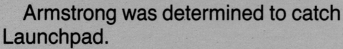

Armstrong was determined to catch Launchpad.

"Try the roof, Launchpad!" yelled Dewey. "He won't be able to get up there."

Launchpad hurried up the plane's rope ladder, certain that the robot was too heavy to follow him. But Armstrong had long arms, and he reached up to grab Launchpad by one foot.

"Let go of me, you monster!" screamed Launchpad.
In a panic, Launchpad grabbed the handle that opened the tank full of water, and watched it spill all over the robot.

When the water hit Armstrong, he froze. Sparks flew everywhere and he clattered to the ground.

"You beat him!" shouted Huey, Dewey, and Louie, joyfully. "You destroyed Armstrong!"

Then they went into the house to free Gyro and Scrooge.

"Great job!" said Scrooge, shaking Launchpad's hand.

"You're not mad because I ruined your robot?" asked Launchpad, smiling. "You didn't seem to need anybody else, with him around."

"I was wrong," said Scrooge. "From now on, you are the only one I'll trust to fly my planes. Agreed?"

"Agreed," said Launchpad, giving Scrooge another handshake.

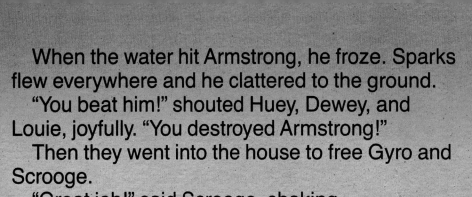

Scrooge turned to his nephews and Gyro. "I've been thinking," he said. "After all this business with the robot, we all need a vacation. How about a cruise to the Bahamas?"

"Hurray for Unca Scrooge!" cried Huey.

"Hurraayyy!" shouted everyone.

EARTHQUACK

Scrooge McDuck had found a series of cracks in the ground around his money bin. He asked the inventor, Gyro Gearloose, to study the problem.

Gyro soon came back with an answer. "I've found a major fault under the building," he said. "If there is an earthquake, every dime in your money bin will be lost."

"Oh, no!" said Scrooge.

"It's okay!" said Gyro quickly. "I've invented a machine that will help. Once we put it under the money bin, there'll be nothing to worry about."

Workers began to put Gyro's anti-earthquake machine in place right away. They dug a tunnel from outside the city to a cave underneath the money bin.

Scrooge and Gyro watched the work. On the last day, they waited at the entrance of the tunnel for word that the anti-earthquake machine could be connected. Suddenly, workers came running out of the tunnel. "Ghosts!" they screamed. "The cave is full of ghosts!"

"Nonsense!" shouted Scrooge.

"It's true!" said the frightened foreman. "When we got close to the cave, we started hearing voices. That cave is haunted, sir!"

"Gyro, bring me a cart," ordered Scrooge. "I'm goin' to find out what's goin' on."

"Good idea," agreed Gyro. "But take along a radio so that you can let us know what you find."

Scrooge climbed into the cart and disappeared into the tunnel.

"Are you all right?" asked Gyro over the radio.

"I'm goin' much too fast!" screamed Scrooge.

But no one heard him.

"The radio's not working!" cried Gyro.

"We'll go help Unca Scrooge," said Huey to his brothers, jumping in another cart. "Come on!"

Gyro waited by the entrance as the boys started down the tunnel.

"The drop is very steep!" warned Louie. "Pull the brake handle."

"I can't!" yelled Dewey. "It's broken! WE'RE GOING TO CRASH!"

Scrooge had already crashed at the end of the tracks. But he was all right. He looked around.

The cave was huge, with gigantic rock pillars that went from floor to ceiling. There were brightly colored balls all over the floor. He stopped to look at one more closely, then jumped back in surprise. The ball had turned itself into a strange creature.

Pretty soon, Huey, Dewey and Louie crashed, too.

"Look, Daddy," said a little being exactly like the one Scrooge had seen. "More from aboveground!"

"It looks like an invasion," said the larger creature, frowning. "This troubles me."

"Who are you?" asked Huey bravely.

"Terrie-Fermies, of course—the people who live underground. You are from aboveground, aren't you?"

"Uh...yes," answered Dewey.

"Leave them, son," broke in the larger Terrie-Fermie. "The Games begin soon, and I am the judge. We'll be late if we don't hurry."

"What games?" asked Louie. But the Terrie-Fermies had already turned themselves into balls and were rolling away. The boys followed them, and found Scrooge in the crowd of spectators. Happy to see their uncle safe and sound, the three nephews joined him.

At last Scrooge understood what the Games were all about. The Terrie-Fermies turned themselves into balls, then rolled at top speed until they crashed against the pillar in the middle of the cave, causing the earth to shake. The one who could shake the earth the most would win the prize—an ancient cracked vase.

"Stop!" cried Scrooge, running to the king of the Terrie-Fermies. "Stop the Games! You're causin' earthquakes aboveground!"

"We must stop this silly sport," said Scrooge.

"But how, Unca Scrooge?" asked Louie. "Everyone wants to win that prize."

"That's it!" said Scrooge hopefully. "Quick! Find one of those mine carts and get ready to get out of here!"

Moments later, Scrooge and his nephews had jumped into a cart and were racing through the cave. They zoomed past the king and grabbed the prize.

The Terrie-Fermies gave chase, eager to get the cracked vase back. But Scrooge and his nephews escaped through the tunnel entrance.

"We can't let them get away with this!" yelled the king. At the count of three, the Terrie-Fermies all rolled together and smashed into the pillar in the center of the cave. The crash rocked the earth above.

"An earthquake!" screamed Scrooge, frightened.

"Quick! Get in my limousine!" ordered Scrooge. To his driver, he yelled, "Follow that crack!"

Scrooge hung out of the window, then yelled again. "Stop! Don't go any farther."

"Are you talking to me?" asked his driver.

"No!" said Scrooge, hotly. "I'm talkin' to the crack! It's goin' to destroy me money bin!"

When they reached the money bin, Scrooge jumped out of the car. Everything was shaking. The walls cracked like eggshells, and his mountain of gold was sliding rapidly into the ground.

"Me money!" cried Scrooge. "Me precious money!" Like water running down a drain, the gold in Scrooge's money bin was swallowed up by the earth.

"I've lost everythin'!" groaned Scrooge. "I'm ruined! I'm poor!"

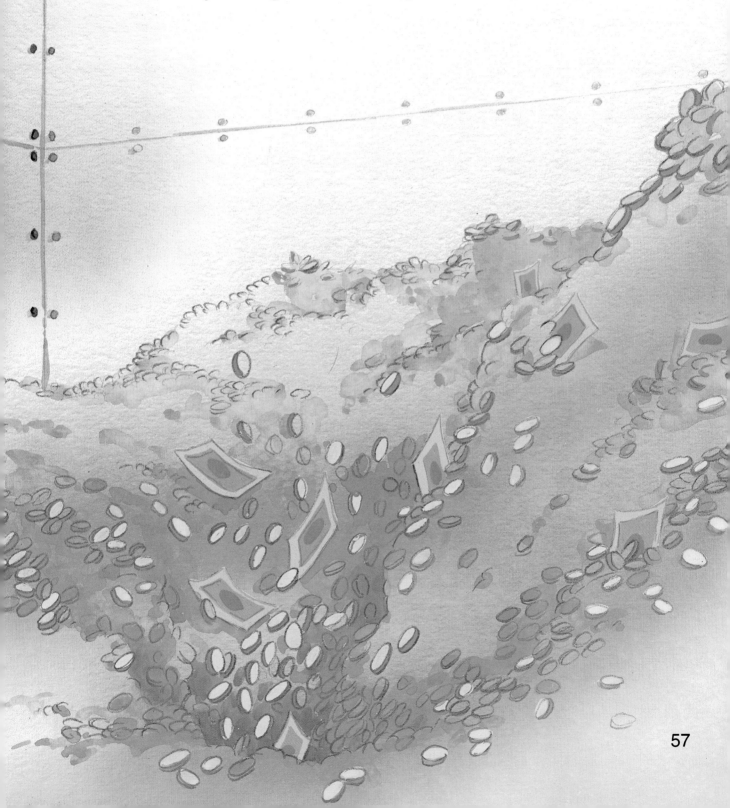

While Scrooge McDuck was crying over his lost fortune, the Terrie-Fermies were up to their chests in gold coins.

"What is this filth?" asked the disgusted king.

"It came from above," came the answer.

"This is awful!" said the king. "They have thrown all this garbage down in revenge for that earthquake. Well, they won't get away with it! We'll send it right back to them."

The quake that followed pushed all the gold coins and dollar bills back up into Scrooge's money bin.

"Look, Unca Scrooge!" cried Louie with joy. "Your money has come back!"

"Hurray!" shouted Scrooge, throwing his hat up in the air.

His top hat rolled along the ground and slipped through a crack, just before it closed up.

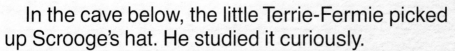

In the cave below, the little Terrie-Fermie picked up Scrooge's hat. He studied it curiously.

"Look!" he said to the king. "The ones above ground sent this to me for our Games prize. It's much prettier than the one we had."

"Magnificent!" said the king. "Now we can really make beautiful earthquakes—not here, though. This place is all wrong now. But I've heard of a place called California."

So off went the Terrie-Fermies, rolling through their caves to California.

Meanwhile, in his money bin up above, Scrooge McDuck could once again enjoy his favorite pastime: playing with his money.